My Furry Foster Family

Buttons the Kitten

written by Debbi Michiko Florence
illustrated by Melanie Demmer

raintree
a Capstone company — publishers for children

The author wishes to thank Melissa Orth for sharing her stories about fostering kittens.

Raintree is an imprint of Capstone Global Library Limited, a company incorporated in England and Wales having its registered office at 264 Banbury Road, Oxford, OX2 7DY – Registered company number: 6695582

www.raintree.co.uk
myorders@raintree.co.uk

Designed by Lori Bye
Original illustrations © Capstone Global Library Limited 2020
Originated by Capstone Global Library Ltd

978 1 4747 8504 4

British Library Cataloguing in Publication Data
A full catalogue record for this book is available from the British Library.

Acknowledgements
We would like to thank the following for permission to reproduce photographs: Mari Bolte, 66, 69; Melanie Demmer, 71; Roy Thomas, 70

Every effort has been made to contact copyright holders of material reproduced in this book. Any omissions will be rectified in subsequent printings if notice is given to the publisher.

Printed and bound in India

Contents

Dad
(Tim Takano)

Mum
(Cindy Takano)

Me
(Kaita Takano)

Eraser

Ollie

Hannah Miller,
my best friend

Joss Lawrence,
Happy Tails
Rescue

CHAPTER 1

New furry friends

Ollie played with a tennis ball in my room. He batted it across the floor with his paws, then he chased it. When the ball stopped rolling, he batted it again. He and the ball went back and forth, back and forth.

"Ollie, stop it," I said, laughing. "You're making me dizzy!"

My funny mini dachshund wagged his tail.

I was sitting on my bed, trying to read a book about cats. My family was getting some foster kittens soon. I wanted to learn how to take care of them. I wanted to be ready.

We adopted Ollie from Happy Tails Rescue last year. Afterwards my parents and I decided to become an animal foster family.

Sometimes animals need homes. Perhaps a family has to move away and can't take their pet with them. Or someone finds a homeless animal. Foster families take care of an animal until it finds a forever home.

I love all animals. It makes me happy to help them!

I put down my book and snuggled

with my old baby blanket. I used
to be scared of things like the dark
or thunder. My grandma made me
the blanket to help me feel safe.
It worked! I'm not scared of those
things anymore, but I still love
Grandma's blanket.

"Kaita! Lunchtime!" my dad called.

Ollie stopped playing. He perked up his ears. He knew that word. *Yip! Yip! Yip!* He ran to the kitchen.

When I got to the table, I cheered. We were having tomato soup and cheese toasties. Yum! Ollie watched as Dad spooned soup into bowls. Ollie always followed Dad around in the kitchen. Dad had a habit of sneaking food to Ollie.

I sat down, and Mum poured me a glass of milk. She and I pretended not to see Dad give Ollie a piece of cheese. When we were all sitting down, Ollie curled up under my chair.

"Are you excited about the kittens?" Mum asked me.

"I am! How many are we getting?"

I asked.

"Five," Dad said.

Five little kittens! I was so excited! I could hardly sip my soup without dribbling. What would they look like and sound like? How big would they be? Would they already have names?

Just as we finished eating, the doorbell rang. *Yip! Yip! Yip!* Ollie barked and started to run to the door.

"Wait, Ollie," I said. I picked him up and kissed his nose. "You will meet your new friends a bit later. I promise." I put him in my room, closed the door, and hurried to the living room.

Dad opened the front door. There

was Joss, the woman from Happy Tails Rescue. She had a pet carrier slung over her shoulder. It looked like a big bag with netting across it.

"Hello, Takano family!" Joss said as she walked in. "Kaita, are you ready to meet your new foster pets?"

"I certainly am!" I said.

Joss knelt down and opened up the bag. Out tumbled four tiny kittens. They mewed loudly and tripped over each other. So cute! One was all white. The other three were orange tiger-striped.

I picked up the white kitten. She started purring.

"Wait, I thought there were *five*

kittens," I said.

Joss peered in the bag. She smiled.
"There are," she said, lifting out the
tiniest kitten.

I hardly got a good look at him

before he jumped back inside the bag. Whoops! Joss reached in a second time. She held the kitten firmly with both hands. He was mainly white, with patches of orange.

"This is Buttons," Joss said. "He's very shy."

The tiny kitten wriggled, squirmed and scrambled back into the bag.

"We've called him Buttons because he is cute and tiny like a button," Joss said. "You can name the rest of the litter. Please use names that start with the letter 'B'. We go through the letters of the alphabet with each foster litter."

I smiled. It would be fun to name the kittens.

"What happened to their mother?" I asked.

"The owners of the mother cat don't have room for the kittens," Joss said. "So thank you for taking care of them. Kittens usually get adopted quickly. I don't think you'll have them for long."

I peeked in the bag at Buttons. He looked up at me with wide eyes. I was going to make sure he knew I was his friend.

CHAPTER 2

Too shy to play

I was excited about naming the kittens. I watched them play, and I watched them sleep. I drew pictures of them in my sketchbook.

The white kitten was the only girl. She was also the bravest. She loved to climb high and then leap into the air, like she was flying. She always landed on her feet. I called her Birdy.

The three orange tiger-striped kittens looked very similar. Each one had something special, though.

One kitten had four white paws, as if he was wearing shoes. As Joss had asked me to pick "B" names, I called him Boots.

Another kitten had a tiny spot of white on his head. It was shaped like a bean. I called him Bean.

The third orange kitten was so friendly. He liked to follow us around the house, wherever we went. I called him Buddy.

I tried to coax Buttons from his carrier, but he wouldn't come out. When I reached in, he squirmed like a worm. He slipped out of my hands and ran back into the bag.

"Let's leave him alone for now, Kaita," Mum said. "Give him time to get used to us."

The other four kittens made themselves at home. The three orange ones climbed up Dad's trouser legs and made him laugh. They crawled all over him. Birdy climbed onto a pile of Mum's books and leaped into the air.

We let Ollie meet the kittens after dinner. I got him out of my room and told him the rules.

"No barking, Ollie," I said. "You don't want to scare the kitties. Please play nicely."

Ollie licked my cheek. He wagged his tail. He was always such a good little boy.

Mum set up a playpen. She put the kittens inside. They mewed and crawled all over each other – except one. Buttons hid in the carrier.

As soon as I put Ollie on the floor, the kittens stopped playing. They watched Ollie, their whiskers twitching. It didn't look like they were scared at all.

Ollie didn't bark. He slowly walked up to the playpen and stuck out his nose. Birdy quickly batted it, and I gasped. Ollie just wagged his tail.

"He's being so sweet," Mum said.

"I knew he'd make a good foster brother," I said proudly.

Mum opened the playpen. The kittens tumbled out. Ollie stood still as all four piled on top of him. They used him like a climbing frame.

I went to the pet carrier and peeked in. Buttons stared up at me. His whiskers twitched, then he scooted back and got as far away from me as he could. He tucked himself into the far corner.

"Oh, Buttons. It's OK," I said. "I'm nice. I really am."

I reached in and carefully picked him up. Once again he squirmed and wriggled. I tried to hold on, but he slipped from my hands. He zipped under the sofa.

"He's just not ready to meet us yet," Dad said.

Mum showed the other kittens to the litter box in the utility room. Dad fed them dinner in the kitchen.

Ollie seemed very interested in the cat food. I wasn't surprised, though. He eats just about everything!

"Sorry, Ollie," said Dad. "I've already sneaked you some cheese tonight. The kitchen's closed now."

Mum, Dad, Ollie and I played all evening with the kittens – except Buttons. He stayed hidden. No matter how much we tried to coax him, he did not want to join in.

I made a tower of pillows for Birdy to climb. She jumped from the top of the pile and landed on the carpet on all four feet. Ta-daa!

Mum dragged a long piece of string along the ground for Buddy. She snapped it back and forth. Buddy got dizzy from chasing it.

Dad gave Bean and Boots a furry toy mouse to share. The kittens took turns snatching it from one another. The kittens were little, but they were so fast!

At bedtime I picked up Boots, and Mum picked up Bean and Birdy. Buddy followed us to the utility room, where the kittens would sleep. Mum and I tucked them in their nest of blankets.

Dad got on his tummy and gently pulled Buttons out from underneath the sofa. Buttons fell straight to sleep with his brothers and sister.

"Good night, sweet kittens," I said, closing the door. The next day I would try to show Buttons he had nothing to be afraid of.

Blankets and torches

The next morning I ran to the utility room. I wanted to check on our new foster kittens.

The door was open a tiny bit. I guessed I hadn't shut it all the way the night before. I peeked into the room and – no kittens! Oh no! They had escaped!

I checked the kitchen and dining

first. No kittens.

I checked the living room next. Thankfully all the kittens were playing on the sofa – all except Buttons.

I went back to the utility room to look for him. He wasn't there.

I looked in the carrier. He wasn't there, either.

I looked all over the house, but I couldn't find Buttons.

Yip! Yip! Yip! Ollie stood in my bedroom and barked at my bed.

"Have you found him, Ollie?" I asked.

A furry tail flicked back and forth under my old baby blanket.

"No, Buttons," I said, walking over

to him. "That is my favourite blanket
from when I was a baby. It's very
special. My grandma made it for me."

I lifted off the blanket. Buttons
raced out of the room.

"Sorry!" I called after him. "There

are loads of other blankets in the house you can have!" I hid my blanket in my wardrobe.

"What are you sorry for?" Dad asked, walking into my room.

"It's nothing," I said. "What's up?"

"I just talked to Joss," Dad said. "She was happy to hear that the kittens are getting along with Ollie. That means people with cat-friendly dogs can adopt the kittens."

"Good," I said.

Dad looked me in the eye. "Kaita, is everything OK?" he asked.

"Buttons found my special blanket from Grandma," I said.

"Oh. Well, Buttons is very shy,"

Dad said. "Maybe the blanket will help him, like it used to help you when you got scared."

I shook my head. I did not want to share my blanket.

Dad put his arm around my shoulder. "Joss told me that it will be hard to find Buttons a forever home if he doesn't like people," he said.

"I know. I'll find a way to help him," I said.

I went into the living room to look for Buttons. Three kittens were playing. Birdy pounced on Bean. Boots chased a scrap of paper. Buddy slept on Mum's lap while she read.

Buttons wasn't behind the sofa. He

wasn't in the kitchen.

"Buttons?" I called. "Where are you?"

I looked in one room, then the next and the next. I finally found him in the utility room. He was hiding under some clothes in the laundry basket. I lifted a shirt. Two big eyes peered up at me.

"It's OK, Buttons," I said. "I just want to be your friend."

I got my sketchbook and sat on the floor opposite him. I didn't sit too close. I gave him his space. I started drawing pictures of all five foster kittens.

I had just started my fifth drawing

when I felt something on my foot. I looked up. There was Buttons! He was out of the basket, sniffing my toe. I stayed very still.

Suddenly Dad laughed loudly in the other room. Buttons froze, his eyes wide. Seconds later he dived back into the laundry basket.

"Buttons, that was just Dad laughing," I said, crawling over to the basket. "Don't be scared. You need to get used to sounds in a house. People make lots of different sounds. Please come out."

Buttons stayed put.

I tried to coax him out with a

string. I waved a furry toy mouse at him. He just dug deeper into the laundry basket. I brought him a cat treat and left it on the floor. He didn't come out for that either.

I looked around the room. I grabbed a torch and turned it on. I flashed the light in front of the basket.

Buttons' nose poked out.

I moved the spot of light to the left and right. Buttons pushed his head up out of the clothes. He watched the light carefully.

Whenever the light moved, Buttons' head moved. He watched and watched. His paws slowly inched up the edge of the basket until…

POUNCE!

Buttons leapt right on to the spot of light!

I moved the light to the door and across the floor. I shined it near the sink and then to the laundry basket.

Buttons chased the light wherever it went. His paws flew. His tail swished. I was so happy to see him so happy!

I moved the light near me, and Buttons chased it. I moved it onto my lap, and Buttons climbed up. His fur tickled, so I giggled.

The sound of my giggle made Buttons freeze.

He stared at me.

Then he ran back to the basket.

"Well, Buttons, I think that was a good start," I said. "We'll go slowly. A little bit today, and a little bit tomorrow. Soon you'll want to play all the time!"

CHAPTER 4

The first adoptions

I played with Buttons as much as I could. He loved the torch! He'd forget about being scared and chase the light all over the place. I always ended playtime with the spot of light in my lap. Buttons would jump onto it and let me stroke him. Our shy little boy was getting braver!

Four days after the kittens arrived, Joss called. She had news. The Kim family would be coming to adopt a kitten. I hoped Buttons would be the one they picked.

After dinner a grandma, a mum and two daughters came to our house.

"We live in a flat that allows pets," the mum said. "Missy and Grace are very excited about adopting a kitten."

Missy was my age. Grace was younger. They had straight black hair, just like me. They sat down with me on the floor. The kittens crawled all over us – except one.

Ollie came over to say hello to

Missy and Grace.

"Oh! Your dog has a cool-looking eye!" Grace said.

Ollie has what looks like a small moon in his left eye. I love it! "We call it his moon eye," I said.

Boots pawed at the toy Missy was holding. She lifted him up into her arms. He purred.

"I like this one, Mum," Missy said.

Mrs Kim smiled. "He looks sweet," she said. "A playful kitten would be good, but not one that climbs on everything."

"If you want a kitten that doesn't climb on everything, you should pick Buttons," I said.

I went to get Buttons from the utility room. The girls followed me.

"Cute!" Grace said when she saw him. She reached out, but before she could stroke him, Buttons squirmed out of my grip. He hid in a pile of laundry.

Grace frowned. "He doesn't like us," she said.

"No, it's not you," Mum said from the doorway. "He's just very shy."

"I think we'll take this one," Mrs Kim said, pointing to Boots. He was still snuggling with Missy.

When the Kim family left, I went back to the utility room. I used the torch and coaxed Buttons into my lap. He sat quietly for a while. Then a lorry rumbled past and he jumped back into the laundry basket.

"He is getting better," Mum said. "We just have to keep working with him. There has to be something that will make him feel safe."

I thought about my baby blanket, but I didn't say anything.

The next day the headteacher from my school came to our house. "Hi, Ms Lord," I said. "Are you here to adopt a kitten?"

Ms Lord smiled. "Yes, Kaita. I'd love a kitten. I have a dog called Milo, but he's friendly to cats. Joss tells me your foster kittens aren't afraid of dogs."

I nodded. "That's right. They love Ollie," I said.

Ollie heard his name and ran into the room. *Yip! Yip! Yip!* He greeted Ms Lord and then followed us into the living room.

Dad pointed to the kittens. They were napping on the sofa – except one. I went to get Buttons while Dad showed Ms Lord the others.

I couldn't find him.

I checked the laundry basket full of clothes. I checked under my bed. I even looked in the rubbish bin! Buttons was nowhere to be seen.

"Kaita!" Dad called from the living room. "Don't worry about Buttons. Ms Lord has picked Bean!"

Oh no! I mean, I was happy for Bean, but Ms Lord didn't even get to meet Buttons. I started to worry that he would never find a forever home.

When Ms Lord had left, I found Buttons on the floor of my wardrobe.

"Hey, you," I said softly, crawling towards him. "What are you doing in here?"

Buttons was lying under the baby blanket I thought I'd hidden. When he saw me, he sat up. The blanket covered his head like a hoodie.

Miaow.

Buttons made a sound! His first one! I grinned.

"Are you saying hello to me, Buttons?" I asked.

Miaow.

He twitched his tail, still under my blanket.

I reached out slowly for him. I thought he would run, but he didn't. He stood still and let me pick him up. I tucked the blanket around him like he was a baby. He didn't jump out of my arms. I carried him into the living room. Dad and Ollie were playing.

"Look, Dad," I said softly.

"Well, I say!" Dad said. "It looks like Buttons is feeling more secure."

"I think he loves my blanket," I said. I sat down next to Dad. Ollie sniffed my blanket and Buttons' paws.

Miaow.

I just sat there on the sofa. I didn't

read or watch TV. I didn't do a puzzle. I just held Buttons, wrapped in my blanket. He stayed in my lap until I had to get up for dinner.

CHAPTER 5

The last one

The next day a university student dropped in to pick a kitten. His name was Anton. Mum told him a bit about the kittens we still had.

I carried Buttons over. He was wrapped up in my baby blanket. "Buttons is very sweet," I said. "But he's shy."

Anton gently rubbed Buttons' ears. "I live with four other people. We can get loud, so I'd like a bold, brave cat," Anton said.

Birdy would be the perfect kitten for him. I pointed to her as she climbed up Dad's chair and onto the bookshelf. She pounced back onto Dad's chair. Her legs and tail waved as she flew through the air.

"Birdy is very brave. She likes to climb things," I said.

"Great! My friends and I go rock climbing," Anton said. My eyes widened. When Anton saw my face, he laughed. "Don't worry. The cat will stay at home! I won't take her rock climbing!"

When Anton had left with Birdy, I looked down at Buttons. He snuggled deeper inside my blanket.

Miaow.

"Oh, Buttons," I said. "We need to find you a home."

After dinner a dad and his son, Karim, came over to pick a kitten. Buddy and Buttons were the only two kittens left. I really wanted Buttons to find his home next. I put him in Karim's arms, with the blanket. I held my breath.

Buttons stayed in Karim's arms! It worked! But when the blanket slid off, Buttons squirmed and twisted. He jumped out of Karim's arms and quickly ran away.

Karim made a face like he might cry. His dad patted his shoulder.

"Maybe Buddy would be a better fit," Mum said, pointing to Buddy. He was rolling on the floor with a toy mouse.

Karim smiled. He sat down and held out his hand. Buddy walked over. His tiny tongue licked the boy's fingers.

"I think Buddy is the right kitten for us," the dad said.

So Buddy found his forever home. Buttons was the only one left.

"This is terrible. What if no one wants Buttons?" I asked my parents.

"Don't worry, Kaita. He can stay with us until he finds his forever home," Dad said.

Two days later Mum came home from work with good news.

"I think I've found a home for Buttons," she said. "A customer was buying a cat calendar, and I told her all about him. Her name is Leah. She seems interested in adopting him."

"Did you tell her how shy he is?" I said.

Mum nodded. "I did. Leah has had cats before. If Joss thinks she would be a good fit for Buttons, we'll have a visit tomorrow," Mum said.

I really hoped Leah would want to adopt Buttons. I wrapped up Buttons in my blanket and held him close.

Miaow. He looked up at me and blinked. My heart melted.

"This is my special blanket, Buttons," I said. "I know you like it, but you have to learn to be brave without it, OK?"

Miaow.

He batted my chin with a paw. For the first time ever, he purred.

***

Leah came over the next day. I handed Buttons to her. He was wrapped in my blanket. Leah slowly unwrapped the blanket to get a better look at him.

Yowl! Buttons twisted and squirmed out of Leah's arms. He dropped to the floor and ran under the sofa.

I shook my head. "You probably won't want him now," I said with a frown.

"Of course I want him, Kaita," Leah said. "I won't give up on him. I promise you."

She got down on her hands and knees and looked under the sofa.

"Hello, Buttons," she said. "You and I are going to be great friends. I just know it."

I showed Leah the torch trick. Buttons darted out and pounced on the light.

"He can certainly be lively," Leah said. "I like that!"

I spread out my baby blanket, and Buttons climbed onto it. I wrapped him up and handed him to Leah. "You can keep the blanket," I said.

"Kaita, are you sure?" Dad asked me. "A few days ago you said you wanted to keep your blanket."

"I know, but Buttons needs it more than I do," I said. I knew my grandma would understand. It was time for the blanket she'd made to help someone else.

"You are very kind and generous," Leah said. "Thank you!"

She put Buttons and his blanket in a cardboard carrier, and off they went.

When they'd gone I gave Ollie a big hug, then Mum and Dad gave me one.

"You did a nice thing for Buttons, Kaita," Mum said. "I'm sure you will do a great job with our next foster animal, too."

"Thanks, Mum," I said.

Fostering the kittens was hard work. It felt good, though, to know we helped all five of them find their forever homes – especially Buttons. I couldn't wait to see what pet came to our house next!

Think about it!

1. How are the five foster kittens different from each other? Include how they look and act in your answer.
2. What kinds of tasks does the Takano family do when fostering rescued animals?
3. Why do you think Kaita didn't want to give up her blanket at first? Why did she change her mind?

Draw it! Write it!

1. Which of the five foster kittens in the story is your favourite? Draw a picture of him or her at play.
2. Pretend you are Buttons. Write a letter to Kaita that explains what scares you and how her blanket helps you feel safe.

Glossary

adopt look after as one's own

bold brave, fearless

carrier box or bag that carries or holds a small animal

coax slowly and gently get someone or something to do something

dachshund type of dog with a long body and short legs

foster being given care and a safe home for a short time

generous willing to share

pounce jump forwards suddenly

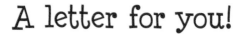

A letter for you!

Kaita Takano, in the *My Furry Foster Family* series, is a fictional character. She is not a real person. However, she is based on a real girl who fosters animals with her family - a real-life Kaita.

Real Kaita fosters pets just like Story Kaita. She also has a miniature dachshund called Ollie. The following is a letter from Real Kaita to you!

Real Kaita loves taking her foster animals to the pet shop to pick up treats.

Eraser

Dear reader,

Let me tell you more about my favourite dog, Ollie! His full name is Oliver Spots. That's because when we got him, he was covered in dapple spots.

We picked him in 2009 — he's almost as old as I am! He was the smallest puppy. He used to fit in the palm of my dad's hand! The spots have faded, but he's still adorable. His favourite thing to do is cuddle. He likes to hog all the blankets. He also likes watching TV and eating. If you don't watch out, he'll steal your snacks! He's an expert at feeding himself.

My mum likes to take photos of Ollie every day. His silly faces make us laugh! Blinking is hard for him. Sometimes he doesn't blink with both eyes at the same time, so it looks like he's winking. In winter he wears a fleece jumper and boots outside. I even have a hat for his tiny head! He doesn't like it much, though.

Happy reading!

Kaita

About the author

Debbi Michiko Florence writes books for children in her writing studio, The Word Nest. She is an animal lover with a degree in zoology and has worked at a pet shop, the Humane Society, a raptor rehabilitation centre and a zoo. She is the author of two chapter book series: Jasmine Toguchi and Dorothy & Toto. Debbi lives in Connecticut, USA, with her husband, a rescue dog, a rabbit and two ducks.

About the illustrator

Melanie Demmer is an illustrator and designer based in Los Angeles, USA. She has created artwork for various clothing, animation and publishing projects. When she isn't making art, Melanie enjoys writing, spending time in the great outdoors, iced tea, scary films and taking naps with her cat, Pepper.

Go on all four fun, furry foster adventures!

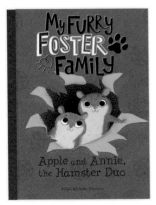

Apple and Annie, the Hamster Duo

Betty the Bearded Dragon

Buttons the Kitten

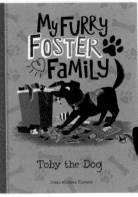

Toby the Dog